BOY FACE

AND THE
TARTAN BADGER

WRITTEN BY
JAMES CAMPBELL

ILLUSTRATED BY
MARK WEIGHTON

Hodder
Children's
Books

HODDER CHILDREN'S BOOKS

First published in Great Britain in 2014 by Hodder Children's Books
This edition published in 2016 by Hodder and Stoughton

3 5 7 9 10 8 6 4

Text copyright © James Campbell, 2014
Illustrations copyright © Mark Weighton, 2014

The moral rights of the author and illustrator have been asserted.

*All characters and events in this publication, other than those clearly
in the public domain, are fictitious and any resemblance to
real persons, living or dead, is purely coincidental.*

A CIP catalogue record for this book
is available from the British Library.

ISBN 978 1 444 91804 5

Printed and bound in Great Britain
by Clays Ltd, St Ives plc

The paper and board used in this book
are made from wood from responsible sources

Hodder Children's Books
An imprint of
Hachette Children's Group
Part of Hodder and Stoughton
Carmelite House
50 Victoria Embankment
London EC4Y 0DZ

An Hachette UK Company
www.hachette.co.uk

www.hachettechildrens.co.uk

MAIN ROAD

STABLES

RIDING SCHOOL

N

THE MEADOWS

MARJORIE INDENT'S HOUSE

CLOOTIE'S HOUSE

WEST CLIFF

SCONE WITH THE WIND

PUB

STUFF

BEACH

STODDENAGE-ON-SEA

Have you read the other
Boyface books? ...

BOYFACE AND tHE QUANtUM CHROMAtIC DISRUPtION MACHINE

BOYFACE AND tHE UNCERtAIN PONIES

BOYFACE AND tHE POWER OF tHREE AND A HALF

Contents:

STRIPE ONE 1

STRIPE TWO 16

STRIPE THREE 44

STRIPE FOUR 80

STRIPE FIVE 102

STRIPE SIX 110

STRIPE SEVEN 114

STRIPE ONE

Some time about now, or maybe a little time ago. Or maybe more like two thirds of the way between a way back and last Wednesday – yes, about then – there was a family. They were called the Antelope family.

The Antelope family consisted of three people who were not

antelopes. Mr Antelope was a large, hairy man who could lift a small car. Mrs Antelope was a large, muscular woman who could eat a small car. Their son was called Boyface. He wasn't really interested in cars. Boyface was a boy like any other boy but more so and different. He was also probably the most perfectly magical child you could ever meet.

The Antelope family lived in a village called Stoddenage-on-Sea, which was a beautiful place in a pebblish cove on the coast. Stoddenage-on-Sea is just around the corner from wherever you happen to be at the moment. Unless, of course, you happen to be in Stoddenage-on-Sea itself, in which case, it's where you are. Don't move.

The Antelope family home looked like it had been knocked together out of bits left over from other houses in a really shoddy way by someone who wasn't really sure what they were doing. This was because Mrs Antelope had built the house by stealing bits of other people's houses and then knocking them together in a really shoddy way. And she didn't really know what she was doing.

Up until the age of ten, Boyface didn't have any pets. It wasn't that he'd always wanted one. He just hadn't really thought about it. So there were no pets in the house. That was, of course, until the arrival of the Tartan Badger.

The Tartan Badger is probably the worst pet anyone could ever have in the whole wild world. It is worse than a smelly dog. Worse than a psychotic guinea pig. And much, much worse than a cat that waits until you've gone out, sells all your furniture and spends the money on missiles.

But when Boyface was handed a Tartan Badger by his mum and dad he was absolutely delighted, even though it was six weeks late.

On the actual day of his actual tenth birthday, Boyface had run through to his parents' bedroom to find that his dad was too poorly to work and that he would have to be sensibly responsible and responsibly sensible and look after The Shop by himself. The whole tale is in the book **Boyface and the Quantum Chromatic Disruption Machine**, but to cut a long story short, that day had been his first day as a Stripemonger. He had learned what he was meant to be and had begun to listen to the voice in his heart.

So when Mr and Mrs Antelope presented him with a bashed up cardboard box six weeks later he had been a bit confused.

'What's this for?' he had asked.

'It's your birthday present,' his mum and dad explained. 'We know it's a bit late but they are quite difficult to get hold of. Literally.'

And they were literally right. The Tartan Badger is one of the slipperiest animals in the whole wild world. Its coat is extremely oily and its back is ridiculously bendy. So it can wriggle out of anyone's hands if it wants to, which it usually does. The only way to get hold of one is to get

it in a couple of G-clamps, then tie it in a knot or put it in a box, which is what Mr and Mrs Antelope had done.

The first thing that hit Boyface as he opened the box was the smell. It was perfectly horrible. A mixture of mouldy lemons and hospitals. A bit like a lemony hospital for mould. The second thing that hit Boyface was the badger's left paw as it punched him on the nose.

'Ow,' said Boyface, sadly.

'Hit it back!' said his mother.

'No. Don't hit it back,' said Mr Antelope. 'It's a Tartan Badger.'

Before Boyface had time to do anything, the Tartan Badger deployed its famous trick. Whenever a Tartan Badger is scared, threatened, bored or tetchy, it will go completely stiff and still so that anyone who didn't know any better would think it was just a stuffed toy badger.

So when it did this combination of punching him and then not moving, it did it so quickly that Boyface wasn't sure what had happened. Looking into the cardboard box it looked like he had just been punched by a toy.

Before he had time to say anything about this, however, the Tartan Badger jumped back to life, leapt out of the box and scuttled up the stairs into Boyface's bedroom.

Since that day, Boyface had been the proud owner of the worst pet in the whole wild world.

There are many features that make the Tartan Badger so difficult to have in the house. Apart from the smell, they have a habit of biting you while you're asleep – mainly on the feet for some reason. Also, they only eat artichokes which are really expensive and can only be bought at certain times of the year. The rest of the year is the time they are most likely to bite you in your sleep.

'It's not even as if you can play with the flumming thing,' Boyface explained to Clootie one day. 'It'll

only let you stroke it if it's in a really good mood and as soon as you think you've made friends with it, it tries to have your hand off.'

'Never mind,' Clootie had shouted. 'Maybe they don't live very long. Maybe it'll die soon like all my hamsters did.'

'No chance,' sighed Boyface. 'Tartan Badgers live for up to forty years. And if you try and give them to someone else, they just run away and come back to you. They need walking twice a day but one of those times has to be in the middle of the night. And he never does a poo outside or in a tray or anything. He will only poo in my bedroom. Mostly in my underwear drawer.'

'Is that why your pants smell of poo?'

'Yes. Well. Usually. Yes.'

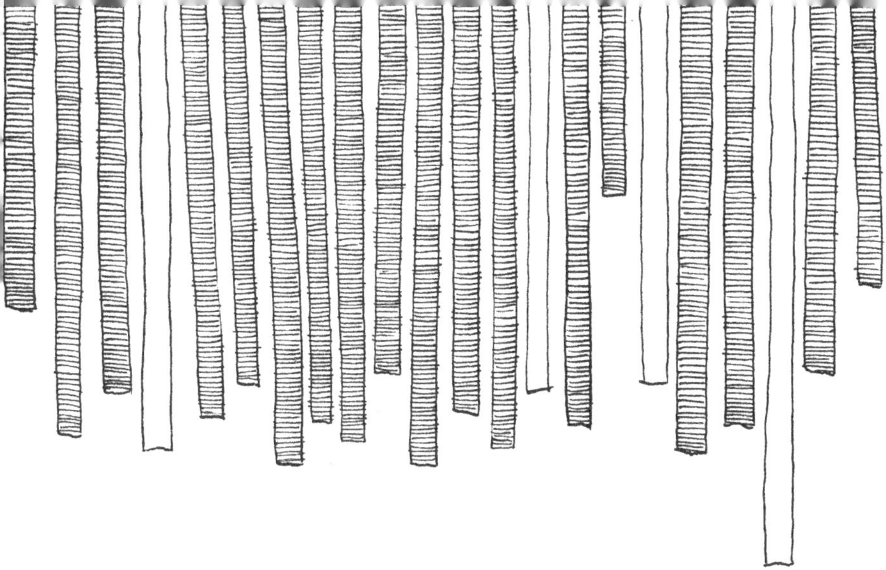

STRIPE TWO

One Tuesday morning, the village was looking particularly sparkly and nice. The sun was bouncing off the bits of boat and sparkly things that seagulls like on the pebble beach. Out in the sea, underwater singing seadonkeys were swimming around, just out of sight, watching through the wobbly waves to see what they could see. Boyface and his dad were in The Shop, doing some work with The Machine. The Shop was like a cross between a factory, a workshop and a massive shed.

If you didn't know any better you would say it was the most disorganised place ever. Towers of cardboard boxes leaned inwards, trying to touch each other at the tops like kissing giants. Buckets of stuff sat on piles of packets of paper and peanuts and felt. Ancient-looking tins and dusty jars perched

on slightly slanting shelves. Orange plastic chairs held together with string and chewing gum made a kind of waiting area. Bubblewrap covered most surfaces and the strangest bits of mechanism filled most of the floor space. Scales of many types. Pincers and hoists. Pulleys and pusheys and roundabouts of rust.

It was a wonderful place, and the place where Boyface was learning the skills of the Stripemonger. They hadn't had any customers that morning so, while it was quiet, Mr Antelope was showing his son some of the features of The Machine. The Machine was looking particularly lumpy that day. Boyface was never quite sure how, but it seemed to have different moods and look different at different times. Some bits changed as well. Every now and again, The Machine would recycle a bit of itself into something else without telling anyone.

'What shall we do today, then?' asked Boyface.

'Well, I've got a box of tennis balls that need using up,' said Mr Antelope. 'We could put them through The

Machine and turn them into baubles for Christmas trees or massive earrings for little girls.'

'That sounds brilliant,' chirruped Boyface and pressed the massive red start button on the front of The Machine. Usually when this happened The Machine burst into life, rumbling and humming in an electric, steam-powered, spellbinding way. But on this occasion, absolutely nothing happened. Boyface froze. Had he broken something? He had been fiddling around with some of

the power settings the day before. What if he'd ruined it? He pressed the button again. And again nothing happened.

'What's going on?' asked Mr Antelope.

Boyface took a deep breath and went towards the shelves to get one of the instruction manuals. 'Well, I think we're going to have to take the power pack off and maybe run some tests on the capacitors. Yesterday I adjusted some of the volt travel of the briochelator and ...'

Mr Antelope held his hand up to gently stop his son from talking any more. 'The thing with problems,' he said, walking around the back of The Machine. 'Is that you can spend a lot of time searching for a clever solution to them. But, often, the best solution is to realise that there wasn't really a problem in the first place.' And with that, he switched The Machine on at the wall and it started as normal. It hadn't been plugged in.

Boyface got his notebook out of his pocket and a tiny pencil that he'd started keeping behind his ear. He wet the tip of the pencil with the tip of his tongue and wrote that down.

Sometimes the best solution is to realise that there isn't a problem in the first place.

Mr Antelope was just getting the tennis balls out of their bucket when the bell above the door tinkled and in came Clootie Whanger.

It was always a treat when Clootie came to visit (if a little loud). She and

Boyface had the exact same birthday but they had only just worked that out. Clootie didn't normally visit on a Tuesday, however. Tuesday was a school day and Clootie usually went to school on school days. Boyface didn't bother going to school very much and never went on Tuesdays. He didn't have anything against schools. It was just that they didn't teach Stripemongering and that was all he was interested in. He figured he'd pick up the other stuff – maths and English and whatnot – as he went along.

As Clootie came into The Shop, Boyface and his dad realised that something was wrong. Clootie was wearing a saucepan on her head. It was completely covering her face.

'Wow,' said Boyface. 'I haven't got a saucepan on my head.'

'Why are you wearing a saucepan on your head, Clootie?' asked Mr Antelope. 'Did you fall into your breakfast?'

'No I didn't,' shouted Clootie from inside the saucepan. 'I'm wearing the saucepan so that no one can see my face.'

'Why on earth would you want to stop people from seeing your face, Clootie?' said Boyface kindly. 'You have a beautiful face.'

'Not anymore I don't,' shouted Clootie, making sure that the saucepan was keeping her firmly hidden. 'I had an accident and now my face looks stupid. I can't go to school looking like this.'

Boyface and his dad looked at each other. 'What sort of accident did you have, Clootie?' asked Mr Antelope.

'I was juggling!' shouted Clootie wildly.

'What the flumming bling were you juggling with?' asked Boyface. 'Melons?'

'What? Yes. That's what it was. Lemons. I was juggling with lemons and I threw one too hard and it hit me in the face. Twice. Melons. Three of them ... Massive ones. Really juicy.'

At that moment, Mrs Antelope came into The Shop. She had been out in the street and had seen Clootie coming in with a saucepan on her head and so she'd followed her in to find out what was going on. Mr Antelope saved Clootie from explaining again by whispering something in his wife's ear.

'Oh, you poor thing,' said Mrs Antelope to Clootie. 'And you're absolutely right. You can't go to school with a saucepan on your head. You'll frighten the small ones.'

'Thank you.'

'Actually, Clootie. I'm glad you're here because I need you to help me with something,' smiled Mrs Antelope. Clootie shrugged. 'I've acquired a red phone box and—'

'What does "acquired" mean?' asked Clootie loudly.

'It means she stole it,' whispered Boyface. 'But stole it nicely.'

Mrs Antelope pretended she hadn't heard him. 'There are loads of red phone boxes lying around all over the place,' she explained with a giggle. 'And no one uses them any more. I thought it would be nice to have one at the top of our stairs. We could fill it with water and keep goldfish in it. I can get it up the stairs myself but I need someone to keep an eye out that I don't hit the walls when I go round the corner.'

'Can I keep my saucepan on?' asked Clootie with a deafening whisper.

Mrs Antelope nodded and took Clootie through the big wooden door that linked The Shop to the house, leaving Boyface and Mr Antelope to carry on mongering stripes. They were a little bit worried about Clootie but they knew Mrs Antelope would look after her. Or accidentally drop a phone box on her head. One of those two.

Boyface looked at The Machine which had warmed up now and was humming and bimbling nicely. It was so clever and fantastical. It could do such amazing things. And he had absolutely no idea how it worked.

There was, of course, the shelf full of manuals but they were very difficult to read; there were thirteen of them and they made Boyface's head hurt. 'Is there any way I can look inside The Machine?' he asked his dad.

'Looking at the inside of the Quantum Chromatic Disruption Machine,' Mr Antelope said, 'is like trying to look at the inside of the Tartan Badger. You have to turn it inside out and it puts up quite a fight.'

'That doesn't sound very nice,' said Boyface.

'Fortunately,' continued the older Stripemonger. 'We don't need to do that because we have an observation panel.'

Mr Antelope pulled a few levers and twisted a big dial and a panel slid back across the side of The Machine, revealing what looked like a cross between a fuzzy monitor and a bendy fishtank. Boyface's dad pulled up a couple of the orange plastic chairs and the two of them sat very close to each other, right in front of the observation panel. Boyface noticed that his dad smelled of soap and the gravy he'd eaten for breakfast.

'We use this,' explained Mr Antelope, 'to see what's going on inside The Machine. Tell me what you can see.'

Boyface stared at the screen. Mostly he could just see clouds. There were colours in the clouds but they were so swirly and unpredictable, they didn't seem to make any sense. Boyface kept

on staring until the strangest thing happened. The Machine seemed to be drawing in light from somewhere behind him. Like an invisible sun was floating in the corner of the room.

The sunlight was casting a glow onto the swirls within The Machine and creating a rainbow, but not an ordinary rainbow. A perfectly circular rainbow. It had every colour you would expect in a rainbow but the central circle was white. And in the middle of that circle was a shadow. The shadow of Boyface.

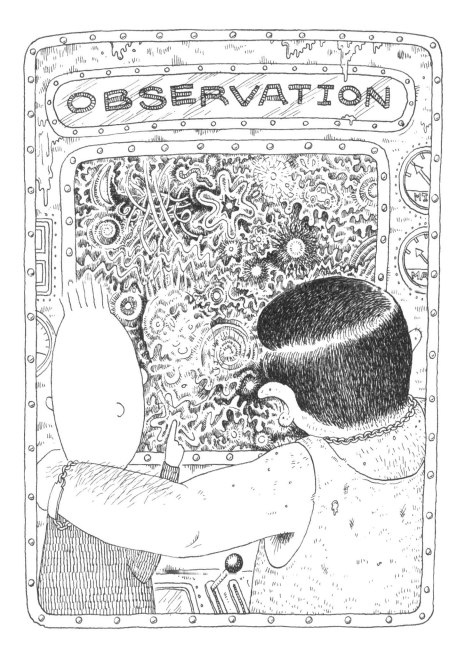

'Can you see the rainbow?' asked Boyface's dad.

'I can,' said Boyface with huge, wide eyes. 'And I seem to be in the middle of it.'

Boyface looked at his dad and noticed there was a blob of gravy on his chin. He thought about telling him but decided against it and turned back to The Machine and the circular rainbow. He looked a bit closer this time and noticed strange blue curls of light that seemed to be dancing and twisting from the head of his shadow. Almost like they were thoughts playing from his brain.

'What are they?' he asked his father.

'Those are the Inklings,' smiled Mr Antelope. 'Not everyone can see them. I remember the first time I saw them and I asked your grandfather the same question.'

'And what did Grandfather say?'

'He said that the Inklings of The Machine are the forgotten adventures of dogs.'

Boyface tried to concentrate on that sentence but it didn't make any sense to him. 'What are the forgotten adventures of dogs?' he said to himself. 'What does that mean?' he asked his father.

Mr Antelope thought for a while, tucked some of his stomach into his belt and said, 'I don't know. Maybe you'll work it out.'

Boyface wrote this down in his notebook and then looked back at his father's chin. The blob of gravy

was still there. Without speaking, he reached out with his little finger and wiped it off. Mr Antelope let out a happy breath. Boyface looked at the blob of gravy on the tip of his finger and wasn't sure what to do with it. It was shiny and he could see both their faces in it. He didn't have anything to wipe it on and didn't want to leave the room to wash it off his finger. He thought for a second and then very tenderly reached back to his dad's face, gently putting the blob of gravy back where he'd found it.

'Thank you,' said his dad. 'I wonder where the girls have got to.'

His wondering was answered by a loud crashing sound and a lot of giggling and laughter. 'It sounds like the girls have dropped a phone box down the stairs,' said Boyface. 'We'd better get a dustpan and brush.'

STRIPE THREE

The four of them soon had the mess cleared up. 'Now then Boyface,' said Mr Antelope whilst putting his arm around as much of his wife as he could manage. 'Your mother and I are going upstairs for a morning nap.'

'We are?' asked Mrs Antelope.

'We are,' confirmed Mr Antelope. 'Why don't you and Clootie take the Tartan Badger for its walk. It's going to need some exercise.'

Clootie and Boyface looked at each other. They didn't want to take the Tartan Badger for a walk but Boyface knew it was his responsibility.

Mr and Mrs Antelope just gave them a wink and went upstairs for their morning nap.

'We'd better take the Tartan Badger for a walk then,' said Boyface, raising both of his eyebrows so high that his eyes went egg-shaped.

'Can I wear my saucepan?'

'Of course you can. It suits you.'

And so, the two ten-year-olds went upstairs to Boyface's room to get the Tartan Badger. When they got there though, they were in for a surprise. The Tartan Badger was nowhere to be seen. The worst pet in the whole wild world had disappeared.

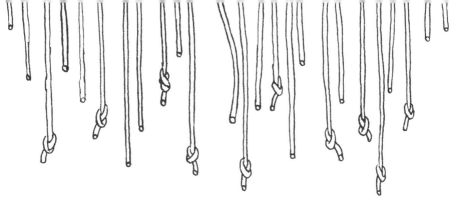

'Maybe it's hiding under the bed?' suggested Clootie.

But it wasn't.

'Maybe it's in your underwear drawer doing a poo?'

But it wasn't.

'Well it must be somewhere in here,' sighed Clootie. 'It refuses to go anywhere else.'

But then Boyface noticed something on the floor in the middle of the room. It was a white postcard. On top of the postcard was a red nose. The sort of red nose that a clown would wear.

Boyface picked up the note and read it.

IF YOU WANT YOUR
TARTAN BADGER
BACK, YOU'LL
HAVE TO DEFEAT
ME FIRST.

'What does that mean?' gasped Clootie.

DEFEAT ME

'It means that someone nasty has stolen the Tartan Badger,' suggested Boyface. 'And he wants us to take his feet from him. That's what **defeat** means. I think.'

Boyface and Clootie quickly decided that they had to find the Tartan Badger by themselves. They thought about telling Boyface's dad but they didn't want to disturb Mr and Mrs Antelope's morning nap.

'I don't think this is a job for your dad, anyway,' said Clootie from under her

saucepan. 'I think we're supposed to defeat this clown note person ourselves.'

'I still think we should ask for some help,' frowned Boyface sensibly. 'The Tartan Badger must be more important than we thought. Let's pop across the road to the café and ask Mr Pointless.'

Mr Pointless was the village's delivery man. It was his job to carry parcels and packages, large and heavy, from the boats on the pier to the shops and

houses of the village. He had muscled shoulders and arms that rippled and popped like ferrets in a pillowcase.

Mr Pointless was usually to be found in the café between his deliveries because his girlfriend ran the place and she gave him free tea and buns. Mr Pointless' girlfriend was called Mandala Eyelash and was probably the loveliest grown-up lady person in the world. She was certainly the most delicious grown-up person in Stoddenage-on-Sea and was almost definitely the most tummy-flippingly scrummiest person you've ever even heard of.

Mandala was a young woman but already she had the aura of someone who knew lots of wise things like how to sit still and when to go to sleep. She wore beautifully soft and floaty outfits that always reminded Boyface of butterflies. She wore crystals dangling from her neck and her hair was always tied up in a bun. Not in the shape of a bun. Her hair was always tied up in an actual bun.

Every day, Mandala would tie her hair up in a fresh bun which she borrowed from the café. The café was right across the road from the Stripemonger's Shop and specialised in cream teas and artichokes. It was proudly called Scone With The Wind.

'A cream tea,' Mandala would explain to anyone who didn't know and bothered to ask, 'is when you get a scone, cut it in half, fill it with cream and jam and more cream. And then some more cream. And then you put it in your face with a cup of tea.'

Boyface and Clootie Whanger stepped into Scone With The Wind. Sure enough, Mr Pointless was sitting at the table nearest the counter looking lovingly at Mandala who was making a big pot of something delicious.

Boyface and Clootie waved hello and sat at Mr Pointless' table. They were just about to say hello however, when they noticed a suspicious stranger sitting at the table behind the door. He was about the same age as Clootie and Boyface and was suspicious for four reasons.

There was a cardboard box by his feet. The sort of cardboard box you might use to carry a Tartan Badger.

 He was wearing a clown costume and his entire face was covered in the weird colours and shapes of a clown face.

 He was missing a red nose.

He just looked like a flumming villain!

The two friends looked at the weird clown boy. He had a fuzzy orange wig and massive shoes. His face was indeed covered with clown paint. But there was something wrong with it. It didn't look like he had put it on to entertain anyone. It didn't make him look happy or funny. It looked more like a disguise. It made him look sad. Like he was hiding.

'Hiding behind clown paint is ridiculous,' shouted Clootie from behind her saucepan. Boyface raised his eyebrows, thought about keeping them there, then decided that would take too much effort. 'That must be the nasty person who stole the Tartan Badger,' continued Clootie as quietly as she could. 'We should go and scrag him!'

'Don't shout,' whispered Boyface through his teeth. 'And we're not going to scrag him. He might be dangerous. Or secretly very nice.'

Through a combination of eyebrow movements and funny faces, Boyface suggested to Clootie that they should

just sit there like everything was normal and see what the weird clown boy did.

'What's going on with you two, then?' asked Mr Pointless.

Boyface used his eyebrows to explain to Mr Pointless that the weird clown boy on the other side of the room had stolen the worst pet in the whole wild world and they had to get it back but that they couldn't disturb Mr and Mrs Antelope.

'I see,' said Mr Pointless. 'Let's have a nice cup of tea and a scone and see what happens.'

At that moment, something did happen. The weird clown boy got up and started getting ready to leave. He picked up the cardboard box (which definitely looked like it had a Tartan Badger in it) and went through the shop door into the street. Just before the door closed, however, he turned back towards Boyface and Clootie and gave them an evil-looking wink.

Clootie leapt into action, her saucepan nearly falling off. 'I'll follow him and find out where he takes the Tartan Badger,' she said to Boyface. 'You stay here and I'll report back.'

Before Boyface could stop her, she had gone. He wasn't too worried though, because rather reassuringly, Mandala Eyelash was coming over with a cream tea for him. He wasn't going to go anywhere soon.

'So who was the weird clown boy?' asked Mandala as she steered her bountiful bottom between the tables like a canoeist.

'We don't know,' shrugged Boyface. 'But we think he's stolen the Tartan Badger.'

'That's a shame,' smiled Mandala brightly. 'Shall we see what the scones say about it?'

'That's an excellent idea,' said Mr Pointless, flexing his arms. 'Let's see what the scones say.'

As well as running the café, you see, Mandala Eyelash also had an amazing talent for reading peoples' fortunes. She didn't use cards or tea leaves, or a crystal ball, however. She used a fruit scone. With this she could tell people about themselves, make guesses at what might happen in the future and reveal amazing facts, most of which involved sultanas.

The process was very simple. 'Would you like me to read your scones?' she asked Boyface. Boyface made a weird face with his face. Mandala took that to be a yes and ceremoniously presented the scone to Boyface on a plate with a sharp knife. Boyface had never had his scones read before but he had seen Mandala Eyelash do it for other people, so he knew just what to do.

He picked up the knife in one hand and the scone in the other and carefully cut it through the middle. 'Try and keep your mind blank,' suggested Mr Pointless in a whisper. Boyface had no trouble keeping his mind empty, it was a skill he'd always had. Sometimes it stayed empty for ages until he remembered to put something in it.

Once the scone was cut, Mandala placed the two halves with the cut sides facing upwards. Her expression changed to one of peaceful attention and she leant over to examine the scones. Mandala never really explained what she was doing during this bit as she liked to keep the details a mystery. Mr Pointless, however, was very keen to whisper a commentary into Boyface's ear.

'What she's doing, young man, is looking for patterns in the lumps and bumps of the scones. She's looking for shapes in the position of the sultanas.'

'Like joining up stars to make constellations?'

'That's exactly what it's like. The bottom half is your past. And the top half is your future.'

'So where is now?'

Mr Pointless stopped and stared at Boyface. He seemed quite taken aback. 'That's a very good question, Boyface,' he said quietly. 'I think that now is in the jam and the cream. But that comes later.'

'So, **now** comes later?'

'Yes. No. We'll talk about now later.'

Boyface screwed up his face. Mr Pointless gazed out the window at the sea for a moment and then looked back at his girlfriend.

'What does it say in my scones?' Boyface asked Mandala.

'Well, looking at the bottom half tells me a lot about you,' explained Mandala. 'This bit of scone tells me that you live very close to here, maybe even just across the road.'

'You know that already,' grinned Boyface.

'And this bit of sultana that is shaped like a baby,' continued Mandala playfully, 'tells me that you are part of a lovely family.'

'You know that my mum and dad are lovely,' giggled Boyface. 'They are your friends.'

'And this group of little holes,' said Mandala, 'Tells me that you are really good at knowing things without thinking about them too much.'

This confused Boyface for a moment but then he realised he was thinking too much. 'Do you mean like the Inklings?' he suggested.

'Exactly,' sighed Mandala. 'Exactly

like the Inklings.' And then she looked at the top half of the scone. Boyface watched her expression and it seemed to change somehow. It was like she was worried about something.

'What is it, my darling?' asked Mr Pointless. 'What have you seen in the scone?'

'This bit here doesn't make any sense at all,' said Mandala. 'There's a hole. Like a place where something should be.' Her brow furrowed and she looked straight at Boyface with clear blue eyes. 'Is there something missing inside you?' she asked sadly.

Boyface thought for a moment and mentally prodded around in his tummy. 'I don't think so,' he said. And then he noticed that there was a sultana on his plate that had fallen out of his scone. 'Maybe it's this?' he suggested politely and popped it back in the hole it had come from.

'Oh,' said Mandala. 'Thank goodness for that. Now it makes much more sense.'

'What does it say now?'

'It says that sometimes the best way to solve a problem is to realise that there isn't really a problem in the first place.'

'Oh,' said Boyface. 'My dad told me that this morning.'

Boyface was a bit disappointed really as he couldn't see what that had to do with the weird clown boy and the missing Tartan Badger.

At that moment, Clootie came back into the shop with surprising energy for someone with a saucepan on her head. With an aluminium clatter she sat down on a seat, exhausted.

'Gosh, Clootie,' said Mandala. 'You look like you've just run up the hill to the main road on the outskirts of the village and back.'

'That's because I've just run up the hill to the main road on the outskirts of the village,' panted Clootie. 'And back.'

'Don't worry about the vase,' smiled Mandala.

'What vase?' wheezed Clootie, tilting her chair backwards on two legs. In so doing, she knocked the table behind her without meaning to. A tiny vase,

stuffed with tinier flowers, wobbled twice and then fell over, rolled off the table and smashed on the stone floor.

'How did you know that was going to happen?' asked Boyface with a wow in his eyes.

'It was all in the scones,' said Mandala Eyelash enigmatically and floated her bountiful bottom back into the kitchen to bake more scones.

Boyface and Clootie looked at each other and made faces. 'Where did the

weird clown boy go?' asked Boyface.
'Did you follow him okay? Has he got
the Tartan Badger?'

'Of course he has. He's a weird clown
boy. That's what they do.'

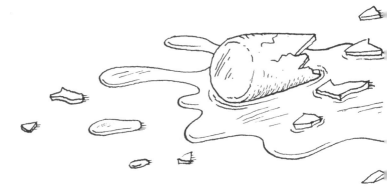

And so Clootie told Boyface and Mr Pointless what had happened while Boyface picked up the pieces of broken vase to see if they would fit back together.

STRIPE FOUR

At the top of the hill on the main road that went past the village to other places was an abandoned restaurant called the Ickle Chuff. It had been there for nearly fifty years and had once been very popular with travellers and some of the locals who wanted breakfast but had forgotten how to make it. Over the years two things had happened.

1. Cars got faster and faster and people got more and more hurried. Eventually, it became really difficult for them to stop because they came to believe that there wasn't enough time.

2. People began to notice that the food was flumming horrible.

After a while, the Ickle Chuff was so quiet it had to be closed down and the building put up for sale. The problem was that nobody really wanted to buy it. Weeds had grown around the building, up and past the

windowsills, and the windows were so encrusted with dirt it was very difficult to see inside.

'And that is where the weird clown boy has taken the Tartan Badger,' explained Clootie excitedly.

'Did he go into the Ickle Chuff itself?' queried Boyface.

'I think so, yes,' squinted Clootie. 'I couldn't see properly because I've got a saucepan on my head but I definitely think that he went through a door round the back. Do you think that's where he lives? No one's allowed to live in an abandoned Ickle Chuff, surely.'

'Who knows?' shrugged Boyface. 'Everything is possible in Stoddenage-on-Sea.'

'What should we do then?' shouted his friend. 'Shall we go up there and scrag him?'

Boyface wasn't really sure what Clootie meant by 'scrag him' but he didn't think it sounded like the right thing to do. He decided to ask for some advice and turned to the village's delivery man. 'Mr Pointless, what do you think we should do?'

Mr Pointless stroked his chin for a bit and then asked some more questions, just to be clear.

'Are you sure he's got your Tartan Badger?'

'Yes.'

'Are you sure you want to sort this out without your mum and dad?'

'Um, yes.'

'Are you sure this isn't one of your dad's tests?'

'No. But even if it is, it's still important that we do it properly.'

'Are you sure the weird clown boy isn't dangerous?'

'We don't know,' said Boyface. 'He does seem a bit odd though.'

'Do you think he wants you to go up there and scrag him?'

'I think he wants us to go up there. He left us this note asking us to take his feet off him.'

Mr Pointless looked at the note carefully then he picked up the keys to his delivery van. 'I'll take you up there,' he said. 'I'm not going in with you. Whatever it is you're supposed to be doing in there, you can do it without me. There are two of you, so you can look after each other. I'll wait outside in the van just to be safe.'

Five minutes later, Clootie and Boyface were looking at the back door of the Ickle Chuff, feeling a little scared.

'Come on, Boyface,' said Clootie from under her saucepan. 'Let's go in there and see what happens.'

With a creak and a puff the back door led them into the inside of the Ickle Chuff. What they found was very strange. The restaurant part of the building was covered in dust and decay. Nothing had been cleaned for years. All the windows were so

dirty that hardly any sunshine could reach inside. The kitchen was even worse. There was a thick layer of oily grease everywhere and it smelled of damp and mouldy hamsters. Looking at the floor, however, Boyface and Clootie could see footprints in the grime leading from the door to the walk-in fridge that had long since been switched off. The two friends looked at each other. They were scared. Boyface reached out and held Clootie's hand and the pair walked slowly to the big door. It was heavy-looking and very different from the rest of the place in that it was spotlessly clean. The door was easy to open and swung noiselessly on silky hinges. Someone had turned the walk-in fridge into a secret place to live. It all felt very creepy and odd. It was full of stainless steel worktops and surfaces which were incredibly shiny and polished. They gleamed under neon lights. The units sparkled. Underneath one of the tables was a perfectly-made single bed: there were no creases in the blankets at all.

On one of the cupboards were some books and some colouring pens.

Another cupboard had been turned into a wardrobe and was full of clothes.

'I see you are admiring my hideout,' said a thin voice from somewhere behind them.

Boyface and Clootie Whanger turned around slowly to see the weird clown boy standing behind them. In the strange light of the shiny kitchen he looked even more odd. His clown make-up seemed to be melting, making him look really sad. In his hand he was holding the cardboard box and it was moving, like something inside it was trying to escape.

'The Tartan Badger must know that it has been stolen and that we are here to rescue it,' said Clootie. 'Don't worry, Tartan Badger. We're here now.'

'I told you in my note,' pronounced the villain, 'if you want your stupid Tartan Badger back, you'll have to defeat me first.'

Boyface looked down at the boy's feet. He was wearing massive clown shoes that stuck out a long way in front of him. Boyface wasn't sure if his feet were as long as his shoes but it was a possibility. 'You have got really big feet,' said Boyface carefully. 'But I am learning to be a Stripemonger. Maybe I could use my skills to help you.'

'What are you talking about?'sneered the weird clown boy.

'Well, I could put you through The Machine and sort of muck about with your feet on a quantum level. Maybe swap your feet for the feet of something smaller. Like a duck. Or maybe my dad could just take your feet off altogether and fill your shoes with expanding foam. Then you would be defeated and we could have our Tartan Badger. It wouldn't hurt. Much.'

'That sounds like a plan,' nodded Clootie, making her hands into fists. 'Or, we could just scrag him.'

'We're not going to scrag him,'

whispered Boyface. 'It's not the Stripemonger's way. Remember that even though he looks weird and sad, and even though he has kidnapped the Tartan Badger, he might be secretly wonderful. Most people are, I think.' He turned back to the villain. 'What is it you want from us?'

The weird clown boy was temporarily stunned and said nothing. But then the box started jumping in his hands and he started talking again. 'What is it I want?' he asked. 'What is it I want?'

He gave a horrible coughing laugh and told Boyface and Clootie what is was that he wanted.

'What I want to do, Boyface Antelope, is make your life a misery. For all of my life all I can remember is watching you and your father and that stupid machine. I've been watching you learning the business of Stripemongering these last few months, growing your skills. I've been watching you messing about with zebras too. And I have decided. I am deciding now. I'm telling you this.

Not this.' (He was beginning to sound like a complete lunatic now). 'I'm going to make it as difficult for you as I can. Starting with this—'

As he said THIS he reached into the cardboard box and pulled out the Tartan Badger. He had tied it in a fancy knot and held it together with two metal G-clamps. The Tartan Badger looked across at Boyface with fear in its eyes. Then it looked at the weird clown boy's clowny face and gulped loudly.

'As you can see, I have completely immobilised the Tartan Badger. He is my prisoner. If you want him back you'll have to come over here and get him.'

Clootie looked at Boyface from under her saucepan which in the circumstances looked like armour. 'Come on, Boyface,' she growled. 'Stop being soft. There are two of us and one of him. Let's scrag him.'

Boyface bit his bottom lip. 'No,' he said. 'I think we should just let the weird clown boy win. He's clearly very clever – much cleverer than we are. Look at him. He's made a baddy's lair here in the abandoned Ickle Chuff. He's found a way to steal the Tartan Badger. I think he deserves it. I'll be sorry to lose the worst pet in the whole wild world, but you can keep it, weird clown boy. You're welcome to it. I hope it gives you everything you want.'

And with that, Boyface took hold of Clootie's hand and led her out of the Ickle Chuff, leaving the weird clown boy grinning with victory.

As they climbed into Mr Pointless'
van, Clootie was very angry. She
couldn't understand what Boyface
was doing and she wanted to go back
and beat up the weird clown boy.
It was a good job she was wearing
a saucepan on her head because it
was hiding her furious face.

STRIPE FIVE

When they got back to the house, Mr Pointless came in with them. Mr and Mrs Antelope had long finished their morning nap and were sitting at the table, laughing at a dreadful cake that Mr Antelope had baked very badly.

'Where have you been, my darlings?' asked Mrs Antelope warmly.

'Oh, it's a long story,' sighed Bofyace. 'I have lost the Tartan Badger. But it'll all work out in the end.'

'It will not work out in the end,' said Clootie through her teeth. 'We shouldn't have left it there with the weird clown boy.'

Boyface told his parents the whole story with help and comments from Mr Pointless and Clootie. 'So what are you going to do?' asked Mr Antelope when he was finished. 'We need to get the Tartan Badger back.'

'I'm not going to do anything at all,' said Boyface with a new confidence that seemed to be growing inside of him. 'I'm going to do nothing, except sit here and eat some of that dreadful-looking cake.'

'You don't seem very worried about losing the Tartan Badger,' said his mum.

'That's because he knows something we've forgotten,' smiled his dad. 'Something that the weird clown boy doesn't know. What is it that you know, Boyface?'

'Well,' began Boyface, swaying slightly. 'The Tartan Badger is the worst pet in the whole wild world. If you try and give it away, it'll just run away and come back to you. Sooner or later the weird clown boy is going to untie that Tartan Badger and take it out, probably to feed it or something. And then what will the Tartan Badger do?'

Everyone realised straight away. One of the Tartan Badger's most annoying features is that if you try and give it away, it'll just run away and come back to its owner.

'The Tartan Badger doesn't need us to rescue it,' explained Clootie, louder than ever. 'It'll rescue itself.'

And just as she said that, they all heard a scratchy fumbling noise at the back door. It was, of course, the Tartan Badger.

Boyface opened the door and squealed with delight as the Tartan Badger lolloped into the house and after looking at everyone like they were the most boring people in the world, it bounded up the stairs to do a long overdue poo in Boyface's underwear drawer.

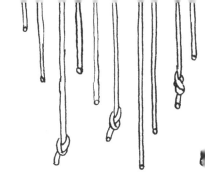

'The thing with problems,' said Boyface, 'is that you can spend a lot of time searching for a clever solution. And often, the best solution is to realise that there isn't really a problem in the first place.' And with that, he took a satisfyingly big bite of cake which was so hard one of his teeth nearly came out.

'Flumming ace!' said Clootie.

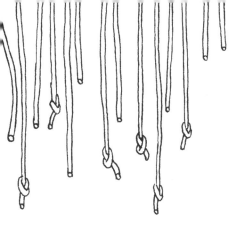

Everyone laughed until their bellies shuddered like tractors turning corners. The Tartan Badger was home safely and everyone was happy. Everyone except …

STRIPE SIX

… Back in the Ickle Chuff was a very unhappy weird clown boy. Of course, Weird-Clown-Boy wasn't his real name. His real name will be revealed in the next Boyface book.

The weird clown boy looked from the empty cardboard box to the Tartan Badger-shaped hole in the dusty

window. Then back to the empty
cardboard box. He'd only let it out
of the knot to give it a stroke. It had
nearly taken his hand off and then
it ran away. His plan had been a
disaster.

He slowly shuffled over to the sink
and ran a dishcloth under the tap.
He took it to the shiniest cupboard
and, using this as a mirror, he
washed the clown make-up from his
face. Once it was all off, he looked
at himself without his disguise.

He had a normal-looking face for a ten-year-old boy except for one thing. He was covered entirely in bright blue polka dots.

'One day,' he said to himself. 'I will finally get even with those Antelopes. One day I will get them!' But then he started coughing and had to have a lie down.

STRIPE SEVEN

That evening, Boyface was sitting on the roof with his dad, looking at the sunset over the sea. The underwater seadonkeys sang each other lullabies but the humans couldn't hear them.

'Have you worked out what the forgotten adventures of dogs are yet?' asked Mr Antelope.

'No,' said Boyface. 'I've been busy tracking down the worst pet in the whole wild world.'

As he said that, a window that Mrs Antelope had bodged onto the roof one time flapped open with a clap and the Tartan Badger came scuttling up the tiles to them. It took one look at Boyface and then bit him on the feet.

'Ow,' said Boyface, trying to get hold of the Tartan Badger as best he could. 'I'm glad I've got it back and everything, Dad, but I just don't understand why I have to be the one who has the worst pet in the whole wild world. What did I do to deserve having my toes eaten? Why can't someone else have the Tartan Badger?'

'Because,' explained Mr Antelope, skilfully taking the Tartan Badger from Boyface's feet and tying it in a knot. 'Because you are the only ten-year-old boy who is patient enough to look after him.'

'Thanks, Dad.'

'And besides,' continued Mr Antelope. 'He plugs into The Machine.'

'What?' burst out Boyface.

'It's all in Volume Six of those books you keep not getting round to reading.'

'Can't you just show me?' asked Boyface with his biggest eyes. 'The books make my head hurt.'

Mr Antelope tutted softly and turned the Tartan Badger onto its back.

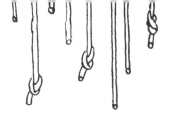

Camouflaged in the patterns of its tartan tummy fur were three shapes like hand-prints.

'Put your hand on one of those.'

Boyface did as he was asked. The Tartan Badger gave a shudder like it was cold, then it went completely stiff and still. Its eyes started rolling around in its head like dice and then some sort of mechanism started up inside it. It was electrical and steam-powered and clockwork and enchanting, all at the same time.

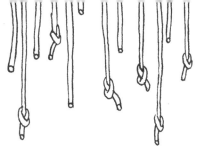

Just like The Quantum Chromatic Disruption Machine. Boyface watched it humming and whirring and bimbling away.

'You can learn to do all sorts of things with the Tartan Badger, Boyface. Think of it as a portable version of The Machine. It's not as powerful but you can do a lot with it. I once made a whole caravan with one of these. So if you end up going on any more adventures, you can use it for Stripemongering.'

'Wow,' said Boyface with wonder. 'That's amazing.' And then he had a thought. He tried not to think it too much, just have it in his head. He was remembering the Inklings he had seen in The Machine through the observation panel earlier that day. 'Do you think maybe if a dog could have adventures it might think up something crazy like a really annoying Tartan Badger?'

'It's a possibility,' mused Mr Antelope.

'So maybe the Tartan Badger is one of the forgotten adventures of dogs.'

'You might be a very clever boy,' said Mr Antelope. He was so proud of his son. 'And also, you might want to think about what the other two handprints are for. But not until tomorrow.' He switched the Tartan Badger off and it jumped back into being an animal and shot off back inside the house. Boyface and his dad stayed on the roof until it was dark.

That night, Clootie stayed on the sofa at the top of the stairs because Mrs Antelope thought it would be nice for her. The Tartan Badger curled up on Boyface's clean clothes pile and munched on some artichokes until it was sick. And Boyface? Well, Boyface switched off his torch, went straight to sleep and dreamed his day all over again.

THE END

Author's note:

Whilst writing Boyface and the Tartan Badger it was my great privilege to befriend Mandala Eyelash. Cafés are wonderful places to write and her cream teas and cakes helped me work through the difficult bits and inspired my creativity. In the course of our friendship, Mandala gave me a hand-written manuscript of her book about scone-reading.

Mandala asked me if I could share the book with other people and so I have humbly included a few pages from the manuscript here. This should give you a flavour as it were, of the ancient practice of Patisseomancy.

PATISSEOMANCY

THE ART OF SCONE READING

BY

MANDALA EYELASH

Introduction To Patisseomancy

Hello lovely readers. Scone-reading has always been a part of my life. My grandmother showed me the basic skills and other teachers have appeared to guide me on my journey along the path. In this book I hope to teach you how to get started and recognise some of the constellations you might see in the scones.

But first things first. What about the recipe? When you are baking scones for reading try and put as much effort and attention into it as possible. Don't do anything else whilst you are baking. Just focus on the recipe and what you are doing. Keep your utensils and your intentions clean and make the very best scones you possibly can.

RECIPE FOR FRUIT SCONES
INGREDIENTS:

50g Butter
225g Self-Raising Flour
1/2 Teaspoon of Salt
30g Caster Sugar
50g Sultanas
150ml milk
1 egg beaten with a splash of milk.

METHOD:

1. Preheat your oven to 200°C or Gas Mark 7.
2. Get everything you need and take a deep breath in, counting to five in your head as you do so.
3. Breathe out slowly while putting the flour and salt in a big bowl.
4. Rub the butter in with your fingers until it looks like breadcrumbs.
5. Add the sugar and the sultanas and mix well. Concentrate on just your breathing and the mixing.
6. Make a hole in the middle and pour the milk into it.
7. Mix together with your hands and form it into a dough. Remember to keep breathing and smiling.
8. Turn the dough out onto a floured worktop and roll out to about 2cm thick.
9. Get a 7cm cutter and cut out eight to ten scones. Think loving thoughts towards them.
10. Take the bits of dough left over, gather them together, roll them out again and you should get another scone or two. These will be particularly special.
11. Grease a baking tray with butter.
12. Put your scones on the tray and brush with the egg and milk. Make them perfect.
13. Pop in the oven for 12-15 minutes or until golden in colour.
14. Say a little 'thank you' inside your head as you bring your scones out of the oven and place them on a wire rack to cool.

Reading the Scone

Once your scones are baked, find a quiet place and choose one to read. Always select the scone you like the look of. Sometimes a scone will chime or sing to you. Place your scone on a clean plate and take hold of a table knife. You may, at this point wish to form a question – something you would like the scone to answer. Alternatively, you might want an open mind and simply ask the scone to communicate to you whatever it feels it should.

Carefully cut the scone in half and place the two halves on the plate, cut-side facing upwards. Once you have settled them, try not to move them.

Cast a gentle gaze over the scone. Spend a few moments quietly looking at the sultanas and tuning into them. Try to empty your mind. Think of it as a blank piece of paper. Let the scone's message write on that paper.

Don't try too hard. Practice makes perfect.
It takes time to read scones and identify the
shapes made. If they don't seem to make any
sense, try changing your position or squint.
Remember that the scone wants to talk to you.
You simply have to learn how to listen.

Very loosely speaking, the bottom half of the scone
represents your past and who you are. The top
half will tell you about your future and what
you could become. The next few pages show you
some of the more common sultana constellations.
The meanings are often different according to
whether you have found that
shape in the top
or the bottom.

CONSTELLATIONS

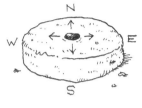

ONE SULTANA.

This represents you. If it is in the centre, you are very balanced. If it is to the north, things are going upwards. South – downwards. West – backwards. East – forwards.

TWO SULTANAS.

One sultana is you. The other is your best friend, partner, sibling or pet. The position of the other sultana, North, South, East or West, tells you how your relationship is going ie up, down, forwards or backwards.

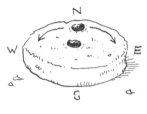

FALLEN FRUIT.

Sometimes sultanas will fall out of the scone and land on the plate. This usually tells you how many children you are going to have.

THREE SULTANAS.

This represents you in group activities. How close are you to others? In which direction are your relationships with others heading?

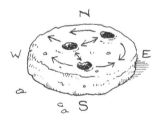

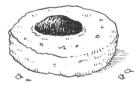

ONE MASSIVE SULTANA.

Massive sultanas have invaded your kitchen cupboards.

THE POO.

Sometimes one sultana will look like a poo.
In the top half this means you need a poo.
In the bottom half it means that you have
done a poo and didn't flush the loo properly.

TEETH.

All of your teeth are going to fall out and will
be replaced by bigger ones. Unless you are a
grown up in which case: all of your teeth are
going to fall out.

SULTANAS PREDOMINANTLY ON THE EDGE.

Friends and family need looking after.
Tell them you love them.

NO SULTANAS AT ALL.

Either it is going to snow today or you
forgot to put sultanas in your scones.

THE GORILLA.

You need to go on a trip to the zoo.

When is it best to practice scone reading?

I like to organise my baking around the phases of the moon. Scones rise much higher when the moon is waxing. I have also found that the bigger the moon, the clearer and brighter a scone reading will be. It is very difficult to practise patisseomancy during a new moon but when there is a full moon you will find the scone will speak to you very clearly. Scones read in the garden by the light of a big, yellowy full moon will give you fine insight into yourself and the world around you.

Find out where the adventure began